Thanks to my husband Emrys

for his love and encouragement.

Text copyright © Linda Owen, 2009
Illustrations copyright © Linda Owen, 2009

Published 2009 by CWR, Waverley Abbey House, Waverley Lane, Farnham, Surrey
GU9 8EP, UK. Registered Charity No. 294387. Registered Limited Company No. 1990308.

For a list of CWR's National Distributors visit www.cwr.org.uk/distributors

Unless otherwise indicated, all Scripture references are from the
Holy Bible: New International Version (NIV), copyright © 1973, 1978, 1984
by the International Bible Society.

Concept development, editing, design and production by CWR

Printed in England by Bishops Printers

ISBN: 978-1-85345-495-0

Robin's SONG

Linda Owen

The shadowy land lulled asleep by the moon
Lay silent and still in a slumbering swoon,
With glittering stars all twinkling bright,
As hushed little birds dreamed dreams in the night.

When the tired old moon sailed away at sunrise,

Blackbird's sweet song echoed out in the skies,

And his mellow refrain began to unfold

With flutings of silver, flourished in gold.

Morning blazed in and chased off the dark

With warblings of Goldcrest, Linnet and Lark;

Bluetit's high calls and tinkling trills

And all sorts of wheezing and whistling bills!

Cheepings and tweetings and twitterings were heard
As all the choir sang ... except one little bird!
Young Robin Redbreast, so sad and forlorn,
Silently listened to songs of the dawn.

Young Robin felt fuddled and full of dismay
As he heard all the cooings and chirpings each day,
For he so longed to sing, and he tried and he tried ...
But there wasn't a peep of a whistle inside!

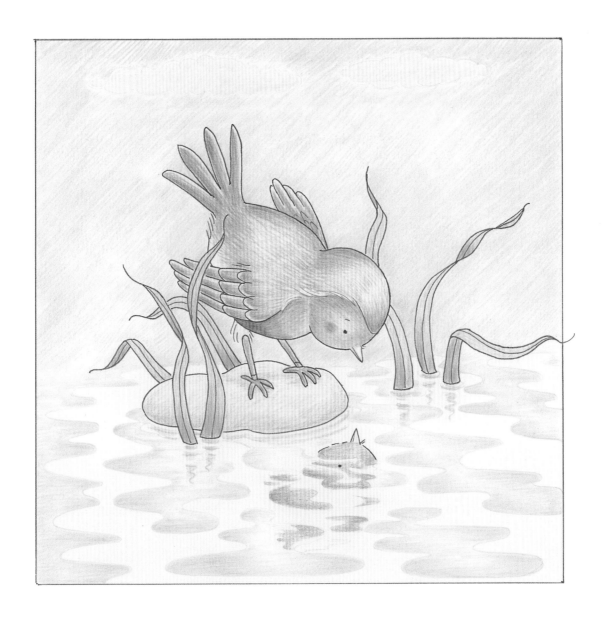

No beautiful song was there to be found,

No crotchets or quavers to warble a sound!

For deep in his heart something was wrong ...

He was weary and dreary and empty of song.

Young Robin preferred to be on his own,
Pecking and preening and perching alone.
As twittering birds hopped up alongside,
He flew in the tangly creepers to hide.

There he stayed for the rest of the day
'Til the sun gave a wink as it sidled away ...
And sorrowful Robin sobbed for a tune,
Deep in his sadness, under the moon.

Then suddenly! Out of the dark, dim night ...

An extraordinary bird, all dazzling white,

With a streaming tail and a spiky crest,

Flew in with a message for Robin Redbreast!

Said the bird, 'I've come from beyond the skies
To tell of the Lord ... who is mighty and wise,
For the Lord made the heavens, the moon and the sun,
The planets and stars ... He made each one!'

'The earth is the Lord's, and everything here;
Although we can't see Him ... His Presence is near!
He built up the mountains, planted the trees,
Scented the flowers and flooded the seas.'

'All creatures are made by the good Lord above
And He wants them to know of His wonderful Love!
For He loves us so much ... and soon you will see
If you say every morning *'The Lord loves me!'*

'And now I must leave,' said the dazzly bird,
'But always believe this message you've heard!'
Then the bird flew away with a flick of his tail,
And all that was left was a luminous trail!

The startled young Robin dashed home to his bed
With the words of the bird whirring round in his head.
And he dreamt that the Lord stayed close to his nest,
Which so warmed the heart in his little red breast.

Next morning as Robin awoke at sunrise

He marvelled at how the Lord lights up the skies,

With the moon for the night ... and the sun for the day,

So all of His creatures can find their way.

As young Robin pondered on all that he'd heard
From the curious, whimsical, dazzly bird,
He remembered some words that he needed to say
Just at the start of every new day ...

So he flew to his secret place under a tree
And timidly whispered, *'The Lord loves me ...'*
Then suddenly, out of the little bird's throat,
Slipped the teeniest ... weeniest ... whistling note!

The robin's heart fluttered as fast as could be,
And again the bird uttered, *'The Lord loves me!'*
Crotchets and quavers escaped from his bill ...
And even a hint of a tinkling trill!

A luminous, whirly wind swirled through the trees,
Ruffling his feathers that fluffed in the breeze.
'The Lord really loves me!' was Robin's clear call,
Then out piped the finest warbling of all!

The robin dashed up to the highest treetop
And he sang … and he sang … and he just couldn't stop!
'Our wonderful Lord has filled me with song,
So my sad, weary heart is now joyful and strong!'

And his beautiful song filled the morning air,
As he whistled his tune with flourish and flair.
The quizzical birds soon gathered around
To see who was making this lovely new sound!

And they all joined in with their chirpings and cheeps,

Flutings and cooings and twitterings and tweets ...

But the sweetest singing that ever was heard

Was sung by that shy little redbreasted bird!

Our Lord reaches down from His heaven above,

For He wants us to know of His wonderful love.

So open your heart, believe He is true;

Our Lord has a beautiful song just for you!

*He put a new song
in my mouth,
a hymn of praise
to our God.*

Psalm 40, verse 3